The Queen, The Bear and The Bumblebee

May 2003

Harold
Love
Dani

This book is dedicated to my two favourite people, Samantha and Nick.
Fortunately for me they are also my children. —Dini

Author Acknowledgments:
I would like to acknowledge those people who helped make this dream come true: Molly
Peacock, author, poet, and mentor, whose friendship and ideas were invaluable. Jillian
Manus, literary agent and angel on my shoulder, who never gave up. Nicklaus Salzman,
whose belief kept him asking, "Mom, is it a book yet?" Sandra and Michael Harding of Self-
Directed Learning, friends and teachers who helped with the language and fabulous ideas.
Rose Cowles who translated my words into such beautiful paintings. Michelle Roehm, whose
contribution as my editor, along with Rosemary Wray, made it even more wonderful. Richard
Cohn and Cindy Black, without whom this never would have happened.

Beyond Words Publishing, Inc.
20827 N.W. Cornell Road, Suite 500
Hillsboro, Oregon 97124-9808
503-531-8700/1-800-284-9673
www.beyondword.com

Editor: Michelle Roehm and Rosemary Wray
Cover and interior design: Rose Cowles
Printed in Hong Kong
Distributed to the book trade by Publishers Group West

Library of Congress Cataloging-in-Publication Data

Petty, Dini, 1945-
The queen, the bear, and the bumblebee / by Dini Petty ; illustrated by Rose Cowles.
p. cm.
Summary: Three friends set sail on a flying red ship into the far reaches of space and through their
adventures learn the importance of believing in themselves and being happy with who they are.
ISBN 1-58270-036-2
 [1. Self-acceptance--Fiction. 2. Friendship--Fiction. 3. Stories in rhyme.] I. Cowles,
Rose, ill. II. Title.

PZ8.3.P475 Qu 2000
[E]--dc21   00-044423

The corporate mission of Beyond Words Publishing, Inc.:

Inspire to Integrity

The Queen, The Bear and The Bumblebee

Written by Dini Petty
Illustrated by Rose Cowles

BEYOND
WORDS
Publishing
I N C

Three friends went out for a walk by the sea,
the Queen, the Bear, and the Bumblebee.
They were dancing and singing their favorite song,
when the Bear said, "Farewell, I must travel on.
I have a red ship that can sail through the air
to the magical land of Who-Knows-Where."

"Oh please," cried the Queen, "Let us go there, too!"
So they jumped on the ship, and away they flew.
The sky was dark, the moon was bright,
the red ship sailed all through the night.
Past dazzling planets they traveled afar
and landed on a distant star.

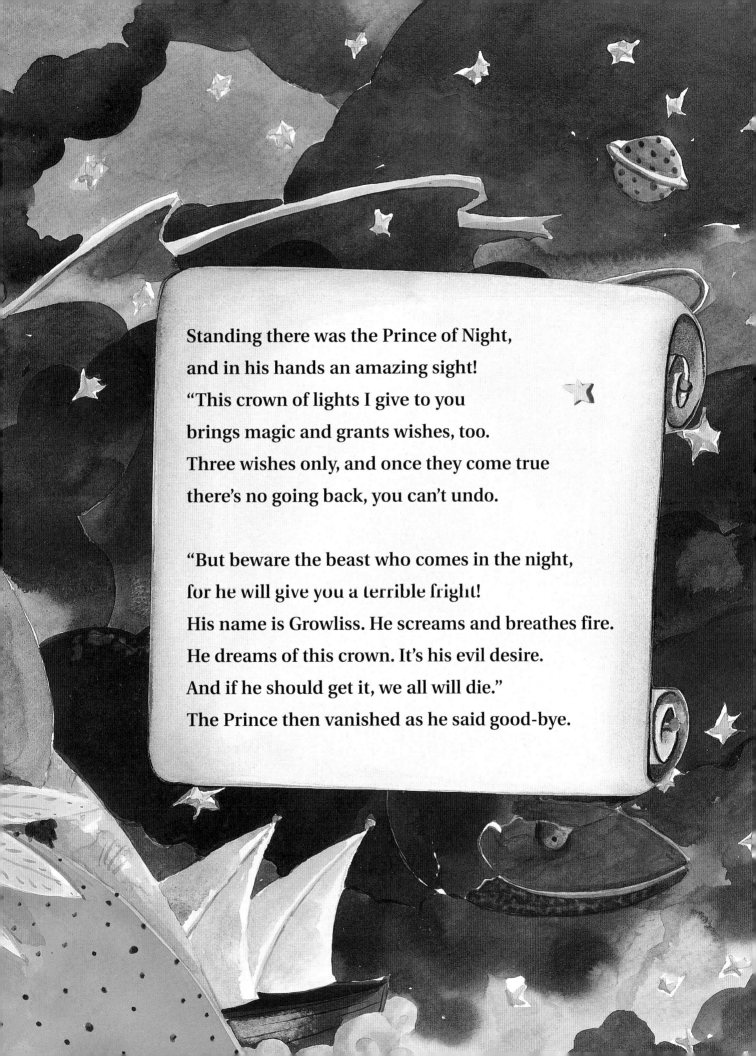

Standing there was the Prince of Night,
and in his hands an amazing sight!
"This crown of lights I give to you
brings magic and grants wishes, too.
Three wishes only, and once they come true
there's no going back, you can't undo.

"But beware the beast who comes in the night,
for he will give you a terrible fright!
His name is Growliss. He screams and breathes fire.
He dreams of this crown. It's his evil desire.
And if he should get it, we all will die."
The Prince then vanished as he said good-bye.

The Queen grabbed the crown and looked at the Bee,
and said to him with obvious glee,
"My dear Mr. Bee, though you are quite small,
your wings let you fly above it all.
I've always dreamed of doing that, too,
so I want wings, just like you."

Before she finished, her wings just grew.
The Queen jumped up and off she flew.
She circled the sky a couple of times,
laughing and giggling and singing these rhymes:

"Oh my, I can fly,
up here in the sky.
Like a bird or a bee,
I can fly, look at me!"

"Oh dear," cried the Bee, "I hope she's okay
and wants her wings for more than one day.
As for me, I can't think of what I will do,
I wonder Mr. Bear, will *you* stay *you*?"

"Oh no," cried the Bear as he picked up the crown,
"I do have a wish." He jumped up and down.
"There's something that I've always wanted to be,
it's really quite different from what you can see.

It's my hair! It's my hair!
It's always just there—
always hanging around
from my head to the ground.
Wherever I go, whatever I do,
I always wear hair, never anything new.

"A man is the thing that I most want to be,
with hundreds of beautiful outfits for me.
I want to wear shirts, hats, tails, and pants,
and change every time I go out to a dance."

As the Queen kept on flying around and around,
and the Man spread his clothes all over the ground,
the Bee was thinking of what he might be,
of how he could change and live differently.

"I know I am small,
I'm not very tall.
Some say that I'm fat—
I don't care about that.
I know if I changed any one of those things,
then someone would say, 'I don't like your wings.'
So I think I'll stay me with all that I've got.
I don't want to turn into something I'm not."

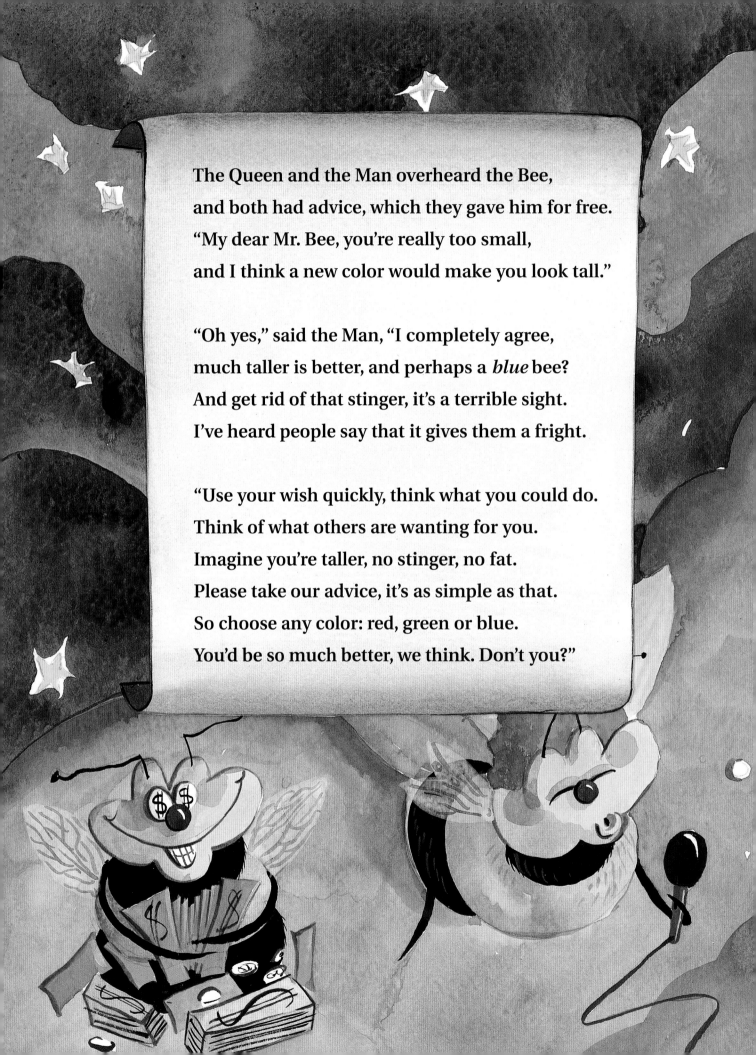

The Queen and the Man overheard the Bee,
and both had advice, which they gave him for free.
"My dear Mr. Bee, you're really too small,
and I think a new color would make you look tall."

"Oh yes," said the Man, "I completely agree,
much taller is better, and perhaps a *blue* bee?
And get rid of that stinger, it's a terrible sight.
I've heard people say that it gives them a fright.

"Use your wish quickly, think what you could do.
Think of what others are wanting for you.
Imagine you're taller, no stinger, no fat.
Please take our advice, it's as simple as that.
So choose any color: red, green or blue.
You'd be so much better, we think. Don't you?"

Suddenly a scream ripped through the night,
Growliss was coming. What a hideous sight!
A nightmare in motion, all slimy and vile,
with flames that slithered out of his smile.

What to do? What to do? They were shaking with fright.
And each of them wondered just how could they fight?

The Man still thought he could growl like a bear
and was certain his old awesome strength was
  still there.
He leaned back on his legs and let out a ROAR!
But he sounded like a man when he lets out a snore.

The Queen, used to having all others obey,
ordered the monster, "Just GO AWAY!"
She flew at him fiercely, but her wings were so new
that she flew the wrong way by a mile or two.

They could do nothing now—this much they knew,
so they yelled to the Bee, "It's all up to you!"
The Bee took his time. "I'll go slow," he thought,
"and it's *good* that I'm small, so I won't get caught."

As Growliss screamed and thrashed in the night,
the Bee looked for a weakness in all of his might.
Then finally he saw it—a tiny blue dot!
Hidden under the chin was the monster's weak spot.

Just then Growliss spotted the crown.
As he stretched out his claw, the Bee flew on down.
Through the flames and the screaming, the Bee buzzed in
with his eyes on the spot under Growliss's chin.
On and on he kept going, all his fear he forgot,
as he jabbed his bee stinger in the tiny blue spot.

Suddenly—silence! The bee hit his mark.
The monster just vanished back into the dark.
The Beast was defeated, they'd won the brave fight.
But things with the Queen and the Man were not right.

"These wings," sighed the Queen,
  "they are always around.
I can't sit, I can't walk, I crash into the ground!
I'm sorry to say I was wrong. Now I see.
I really would rather be just good old me."

"Me too," cried the Man, as he took off his shirt.
"I never once thought of the work or the dirt
that comes with these clothes. They just aren't for me!
I want to be hairy and scary and free."

The Prince reappeared to tell them the worst,
"I'm sorry, but some things just can't be reversed."

"'Scuse me," said the Bee, "but there's one wish to go.
And what I desire, I most certainly know.
Please change my friends back to the same old way
they were before this long magic day."

The Bee's wish was granted because fair is fair.
The Queen lost her wings, and the Bear got his hair.
And both of them learned that the best thing to do
is be who you are—'cause there's only one you!